EARTH DAY
FROM THE
BLACK LAGOON®

Get more monster-sized laughs from

The Black Lagoon®

MOON

CHOCOLATE-CHIP COOKIE

EARTH DAY
FROM THE
BLACK LAGOON®

I NEED A PIT STOP.

by Mike Thaler
Illustrated by Jared Lee

SCHOLASTIC INC.

For Jared:
30 years—the best!
—M.T.

To Jack and June Schneider
—J.L.

SPACE
SNAKE

ISBN 978-0-545-47669-0

Text copyright © 2013 by Mike Thaler
Illustrations copyright © 2013 by Jared D. Lee Studio, Inc.

12 11 10 9 8 7 6 5 4 3 2 1   13 14 15 16 17 18/0

Printed in the U.S.A.   40
First printing, March 2013

PLASTIC
SKULL

← STAR

CONTENTS

 ← PLANET

CHAPTER 1
GREEN FOR GREEN

When Mrs. Green announced that in two weeks we would celebrate Earth Day, everyone was very excited. Then when she said in preparation we would all have to do reports on special topics, everyone sighed.

She wrote a long list on the board. At least we could choose our topic.

SNACK

Eric took *endangered species* because he felt class clowns were an endangered species.

Freddy took *food supply*, a subject close to his heart.

Derek took *recycling* because he thought it was about bike riding.

I'VE ALWAYS WANTED TO RIDE A UNICYCLE.

Randy took *global warming* because he thought it was a hot topic.

THE ARCTIC OCEAN IS AS WARM AS BATHWATER.

Doris took *air pollution*, even
though she thought it was un-
ladylike.

Penny took *solutions* because
she's a show-off.

And I was left with *water pollution.*

Eric snickered, "Looks like you're all wet, Hubie!"

CHAPTER 2
READ IT AND WEEP

Next, we all went to the library to do research. We looked in the nonfiction section because all these problems are very real!

I felt bad when I read how so many of our rivers, lakes, and even our oceans have been poisoned by pollution. We were all upset on the bus ride home that day.

CHAPTER 3
EVERY LITTER BIT HURTS

"Don't grown-ups care, Mom, what kind of world they're leaving us kids?"

16

"It's not just grown-ups, Hubie, it's everyone. When you run the water as you're brushing your teeth, that's wasteful. When you throw a soda can in the regular trash, that's wasteful. When you throw paper on the ground, that's pollution. It all adds up."

17

"You're right, Mom. I'm going to turn over a new leaf . . . a green leaf."

NEW LEAF

THIS MEANS HUBIE IS GOING TO START BEHAVING IN A BETTER WAY.

EXACT SIZE

I'M GOING TO RECYCLE MY BOOGERS.

CHAPTER 4
THE NEW HUBIE

Hubie started by cleaning up his room. Then he went outside and swept up his whole street. He started one recycling bin for aluminum and plastic, one for glass, and one for paper. The world felt better already.

BE BACK FOR DINNER.

OK.

TOXIC RAIN →

CHAPTER 5
NO NEWS IS BAD NEWS

The next day, everyone gave their reports. Hubie learned a lot. There are places where the tallest mountains are made of garbage.

In the ocean, there are giant islands made of plastic. Soon all the rivers, streams, and lakes will be polluted, and even the rain will be toxic. In years to come there may not be enough food for everyone. And what there is could be poisoned.

DOG WORM

23

Just then the lunch bell rang, and everyone rushed off to lunch, laughing. Everyone except Hubie. He was the only one who took it seriously.

UNICYCLE →

CHAPTER 6
HUBIE THE
RE-CYCLONE

The new, recycled Hubie stood in the cafeteria line.

"Only take what you're going to eat," he told the kids standing in front of him. "Finish everything you take," he told the kids standing behind him.

WHO MADE YOU THE FOOD COP?

No one listened.

When lunch was finished, there were still mounds of unfinished food left on the plates. So Hubie brought out his secret weapon: Freddy.

Freddy finished everything and licked the plates.

"Waste not, want not," said Hubie.

CHAPTER 7
DREAM CLOUDS

That night, Hubie had a
nightmare. He woke up and
the sky was dark. Big clouds of
smoke covered the sun. He got
dressed and went out to climb
a tree, but he couldn't find one.

CHAPTER 7
DREAM CLOUDS

That night, Hubie had a
nightmare. He woke up and
the sky was dark. Big clouds of
smoke covered the sun. He got
dressed and went out to climb
a tree, but he couldn't find one.

I'M BORED.

I CAN ALWAYS EAT YOU.

There weren't any flowers, either. In fact, there was nothing green to be seen. The ground was as gray as the sky, and there was no difference between night and day.

MIKE THALER
HAVING A
GLOOMY DAY →

31

He woke up and ran to the
window. The sun was just coming
up and its light began to warm

the earth. All the flowers turned to welcome it, and the birds sang their thanks for a brand-new day.

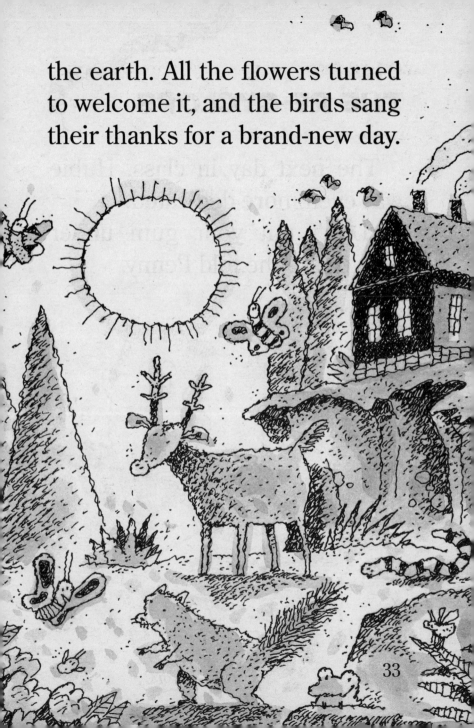

CHAPTER 8
THE RE-CYCLOPS

The next day in class, Hubie was even more dedicated.

"Don't put your gum under your desk!" he told Penny.

"Don't waste that piece of paper," he told Eric.

"Recycle your eraser crumbs," he told Derick.

He opened all the windows. He turned off all the lights. He even told Mrs. Green not to give so much homework because everyone would have to stay up late and use lots of electricity.

TURN THE LIGHTS BACK ON AND SIT DOWN.

HOMEWORK IS A WASTE OF PAPER.

It was clear that they had created a Re-cyclops monster.

CHAPTER 9

OFF THE DEEP END

At home, Hubie was even worse. He put a sail on the car. He hooked up a lightbulb to the hamster wheel. He wouldn't take a bath Friday night because it would waste water. He even thought about taking the aluminum siding off their house to recycle it. Hubie was going to save the world. He felt like a superhero!

HUBIE, COME ON. THE WATER IS NICE AND HOT.

MAKE ROOM FOR ME.

CHAPTER 10
RECYCLE MAN

Faster than a rolling aluminum can.

Able to leap piles of garbage in a single bound.

It's a word.
It's a plan.
It's Recycle Man.

A group of unthinking school kids are about to drop their ice-cream wrappers on the ground, but before they can, Recycle Man brings in a garbage can.

"The can can," he tells them, "make a cleaner, healthier, safer environment."

41

"Hubie, wake up! We're at school," says T-Rex.

"Huh, huh, oh. T-Rex, turn off the engine. You're wasting gas and polluting the air!"

SCHOOL

PLEASE GET OUT.

43

CHAPTER 11
PRESENTS OF MIND

"Well, class, tomorrow is Earth Day, and I'd like you each to bring in a present for Mother Earth," announced Mrs. Green.

Everybody scratched their head. Hubie took out a pencil and started writing.

CHAPTER 12
EARTH MIRTH

It was Friday, and everyone was very excited.

Doris did a dance for Mother Earth.

WHAT GRACE.

WHAT FORM.

I'M SO MOVED.

OH, BROTHER.

46

Eric asked ecology riddles.*

Randy made a wastebasket out of a large tin can.

"It's your turn, Hubie," said Mrs. Green.

Hubie stepped to the front of the class and cleared his throat. "A poem," he announced.

← DOG ALLERGIC TO FROGS

49

A FEW EARTH FACTS

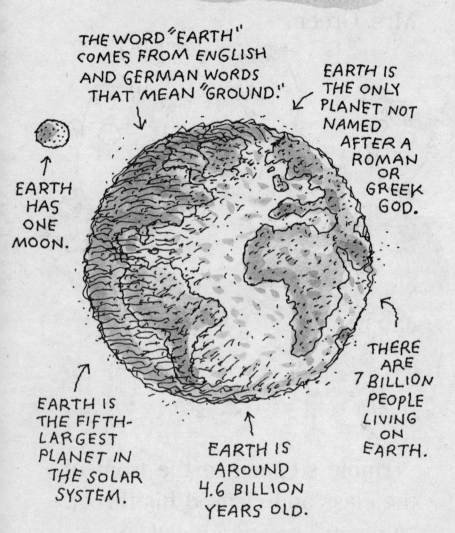

THE WORD "EARTH" COMES FROM ENGLISH AND GERMAN WORDS THAT MEAN "GROUND."

EARTH IS THE ONLY PLANET NOT NAMED AFTER A ROMAN OR GREEK GOD.

EARTH HAS ONE MOON.

EARTH IS THE FIFTH-LARGEST PLANET IN THE SOLAR SYSTEM.

EARTH IS AROUND 4.6 BILLION YEARS OLD.

THERE ARE 7 BILLION PEOPLE LIVING ON EARTH.

CHAPTER 13
FOR MOTHER EARTH

SNACK

Dear Earth Mother,
You are so great.
We have no other.
You give us everything we
     need,
But we need to take heed.

WOULD YOU LIKE A RIDE?

NO, THANKS, I'LL JUST KEEP ON ROLLING.

If we are careless with
  pollution,
We will be airless, with no
  solution.
If we are sloppy with our waste,
Our water will have a funny
  taste.
Unless we have more car pools,
We will run out of fuels.
We all need to take more care,
So when we grow up
You'll still be there.

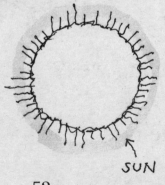

SUN

THE SUN IS
93 MILLION
MILES
FROM
EARTH.

EARTH

52

IN THE MIDDLE AGES, PEOPLE THOUGHT THE EARTH WAS FLAT.

I'M SO BORED ON THIS PAGE.

CHAPTER 14
ACTIONS SPEAK AS LOUD AS WORDS

Everyone sat with their mouths open as Hubie sat down.

Then, one by one, they started to applaud till the whole class was standing up and cheering.

"Well," said Hubie, "let's all go out and pick up trash."
And they did.

56

And that's how they celebrated Earth Day!

ERIC'S ECOLOGY RIDDLES

1. When is the earth sad?
When it's down in the dumps.

WHY THE FROWN?

2. What do you call it when the air is filled with rabbits?
Hare pollution.

3. When is a boat cheapest to buy?
When it's on sail.

4. What do you call a sun-powered tooth?

A solar molar.

5. What one habit does every creature on earth share?

Our habit-tat.

6. What nation can change the world?

Your imagi-nation.

HMMM.

7. What race is everyone in?
The human race.

8. Where do you mail organic garbage?
At the compost office.

9. What three letters run everything?
N R G.

10. What is recycling?
A pollution solution.

11. Why was Doctor Frankenstein an environmentalist?
Because he made his monster from recycled parts.

12. How can the earth get in shape?
By reducing its waist.

13. What ability does everyone on earth have to help the environment?

Response-ability.

14. What kind of vehicle can we all ride to a better life?

A re-cycle.

15. "Knock, knock."
"Who's there?"
"Trash can."
"Trash can who?"
"Trash can ruin the world."

16. "Knock, knock."
"Who's there?"
"Garden."
"Garden who?"
"Garden the environment is important."

And remember—to save our planet, plan it!

  WE CAN ALL PITCH IN.